God is Good to Me

by Thais Clemente Lima

TATE PUBLISHING & Enterprises

S0-AWQ-613

God is Good to Me
Copyright © 2010 by Thais Clemente Lima. All rights reserved.

This title is also available as a Tate Out Loud product.
Visit www.tatepublishing.com for more information.

No part of this publication may be reproduced, stored in a retrieval system or transmitted in any way by any means, electronic, mechanical, photocopy, recording or otherwise without the prior permission of the author except as provided by USA copyright law.

The opinions expressed by the author are not necessarily those of Tate Publishing, LLC.

Published by Tate Publishing & Enterprises, LLC
127 E. Trade Center Terrace | Mustang, Oklahoma 73064 USA
1.888.361.9473 | www.tatepublishing.com

Tate Publishing is committed to excellence in the publishing industry. The company reflects the philosophy established by the founders, based on Psalm 68:11,
"The Lord gave the word and great was the company of those who published it."

Book design copyright © 2010 by Tate Publishing, LLC. All rights reserved.
Cover and interior design by Elizabeth M. Hawkins
Illustrations by Glori Alexander

Published in the United States of America

ISBN: 978-1-61739-088-3
1. Juvenile Fiction / Religious / Christian / General
2. Ages 0-3
10.08.17

To Laura and Hugo.

Petita woke up excited. She loved to play in the backyard with her little brother, Nico, and the sunny Saturday was just perfect!

"Good, good morning, Mom!" said Petita with a huge smile.

"Good morning, Petita!"

Petita kept walking and talking. "Good, good morning, Dad!"

She didn't hear an answer and said it louder. "Good, good, good morning, Dad!"

She still didn't hear her dad responding, but now her mom said, "Petita, Daddy went out to get milk. He will be back soon."

"Okay. Good, good morning, Nico!" Petita saw her little brother leaving his room.

"Good, good morning, everyone!" yelled Petita. "Good, good, good morning." Then she went down through the kitchen door to the backyard.

"Hey, Petita, brush your teeth first, please!" her mom reminded her.

"No! I want to go outside!"

Her mom walked with her to the washroom, explaining that we have to brush our teeth to keep them healthy. Petita brushed her teeth, complaining. "Why? Why? Why? Why?"

"God made our teeth so we could eat the wonderful food He provides that helps us grow big and strong. We were made in His image, and our body is a temple, so we should take good care of it to show God how much we love Him."

"Okay. Okay. You are right!"

The grumpy little face smiled again once Petita saw her dad arriving. "Good, good morning, Dad!" She rushed to give him a hug and started asking, "What did you buy? Where is it? Where? Where? Where?" She ran to go outside again.

"Wait! You've got to slow down," said her dad. "Let's sit down and have breakfast first."

"No! I want to go outside! Why? Why? Why? Why?"

Petita's questions never ended. Her parents did not know what to do with so many questions. She was very curious and asked about everything and everyone.

Petita did have breakfast with her little brother, Nico, and soon went to the backyard. It certainly was a beautiful, sunny day. Petita and her little brother were having a great time playing in the sand box.

"What a beautiful blue sky!" Petita was saying enthusiastically. "What a bright sun! Look at all these birds flying back and forth." Petita could not stop.

"Dad!" screamed Petita. "Why is the sky blue? Why is the sun hot? Why is the grass green? Why? Why? Why? Why?"

Her dad was about to give up on answering any questions she had—it was certainly confusing trying to answer them all. He then decided to try something else. He went back inside and brought his Bible to share a story with Petita.

"Petita, sweetheart, come here. I want to tell you a story from the Bible," said her dad.

He opened the Bible right at the beginning, in Genesis 1, and started reading. "In the beginning God created the heavens and the earth."

"God created the heavens and the earth?" asked Petita.

"Yes. God created the heavens and the earth. Everything was dark and God said: Let there be light; and there was light. That was the first day. God created day and night."

Again, Petita could not keep it to herself and asked, "God created day and night?"

"Yes."

"Wait a minute! God is good to me! God is good to me!" she sang.

Her dad smiled back at her and continued reading. "On the second day, God separated the sky from the water. On the third day, God separated dry ground from the water. And that's exactly what happened. God called the dry ground land and the water ocean."

"Wait a minute! God created the beautiful and big, blue ocean? And the land?"

"Yes!"

"God is good to me! God is good to me!" she kept singing.

Her dad continued the reading. "And the land produced trees, which produced fruits."

"Wait a minute! God created the plants and the fruits?"

"Yes!"

"God is good to me! God is good to me!"

Her dad kept reading Genesis 1, telling Petita that God also created the sun, the moon, and stars. He mentioned that God also created all the animals and He specially created man and woman, boys and girls.

"Why is God so good to me?"

"That is because He loves you so, so much!"

She danced and sang in happiness, knowing how God is good to her. She was incredibly happy to get so many answers to her questions, and, more importantly, she was happy that God created her too.

Isn't it good? God also created you and me.

God is good to us!

e|LIVE

listen|imagine|view|experience

AUDIO BOOK DOWNLOAD INCLUDED WITH THIS BOOK!

In your hands you hold a complete digital entertainment package. In addition to the paper version, you receive a free download of the audio version of this book. Simply use the code listed below when visiting our website. Once downloaded to your computer, you can listen to the book through your computer's speakers, burn it to an audio CD or save the file to your portable music device (such as Apple's popular iPod) and listen on the go!

How to get your free audio book digital download:

1. Visit www.tatepublishing.com and click on the e|LIVE logo on the home page.
2. Enter the following coupon code:
   8047-3770-86b5-5230-1cfa-2074-0e5a-e989
3. Download the audio book from your e|LIVE digital locker and begin enjoying your new digital entertainment package today!